To my parents, who have always told the best stories, to my sister Fran, and to Ted.—L.M.

For Roxanne.—D.D.

Text © 1991, Linda Lowe Morris
Illustrations © 1991, David DeRan
Published by Picture Book Studio, Saxonville, MA.
All rights reserved.
Printed in Hong Kong.
10 9 8 7 6 5 4 3 2 1

Library of Congress Cataloging in Publication Data
Morris, Linda Lowe.
Morning milking / by Linda Lowe Morris ; illustrated by David DeRan
Summary: A young girl who spends her mornings helping her father milk the cows
in the barn tries to stop time so that she can hold onto each vivid moment.
ISBN 0-88708-173-8 : $16.95
[1. Milking—Fiction. 2. Farm life—Fiction.] I. DeRan, David, ill. II. Title.
PZ7.M82835Mo 1991
[E]—dc20 91-13103

Ask your bookseller for other fine books from Picture Book Studio.

Morning Milking

LINDA LOWE MORRIS   DAVID DERAN

PICTURE BOOK STUDIO

From somewhere deep inside my dream I hear a sound. It's coming closer, getting louder and louder, but there's nothing I can do.

In a blink, the dream melts away and I am back in my own warm bed surrounded by the softness of pillows and covers.

Now I know the sound. It's the sound of the alarm clock buzzing—not my alarm but my father's, coming from my parents' room across the hall. I hear a click now and it stops.

Outside my window I can see it's still dark. A sliver of moon hangs low in the sky. But I hear my father getting out of bed. For him it's the beginning of the day—the time when he goes down to the barn to milk the cows.

I listen to the soft rustling sounds of my father getting dressed. Everything else in the house is quiet. My mother and my sister must still be sleeping.

My sister, who is three years older, never goes out to the barn in the morning. She and I have silently staked out our separate claims here on the farm. She has the house, her books, her magazines, her music. I have the woods, the creek that runs down through the meadow, the barn—and the cows. I claim the cows as mine.

Sleep tugs hard at my arms and legs but I fight it. I know if I can wake up enough to get out of bed, I can go out to the barn with my father.

As he goes down the stairs, I know he'll soon be out the door so I quickly crawl out from under the covers and begin getting dressed.

A few minutes later I walk into the bright light of the kitchen. It smells of hot coffee and toasted raisin bread. Skippie, our dog, gets up off the floor and comes over to me and I reach down and scratch his ears.

"Hi, Pop," I say to my father, who is sitting at the table.

He smiles, just a little.

"What are you doing up?" he says, as he always does.

I shrug my shoulders.

"I don't know," I say, but I do. We milk the cows both morning and evening, but I love morning milking most of all. It seems like the whole world's asleep but me and Pop.

He stands up and now I have to hurry. I drop a slice of raisin bread in the toaster and run to the closet. I throw on my coat, wrap a scarf around my neck and pull on my hat. Then I run back and grab the toast just in time to follow him out the door.

It snowed during the night, an inch or so, just enough to coat the ground with dry white powder and muffle our footsteps over the gravel.

But now the sky has cleared, and in the stillness, each breath I take feels needle-sharp.

Skippie runs alongside us snorting and sniffing. He rubs his nose in the snow, rolls over in it and jumps up again. He stops to shake himself. Then, wagging his tail, he runs circles around us, weaving back and forth between my father and me.

From out in the barn come sounds like little bells, the jingling of the number tags the cows wear around their necks.

I stop and look up at the sky—deep blue-black on this nearly moonless morning, with so many stars there is hardly room for sky in between. I hold every muscle still and stare at them hard. And for a moment, I am only my eyes—only my eyes and the stars.

Some of the stars are bright and twinkly. As I watch, even more appear, some so far away they don't look like stars anymore, just tiny little smudges up in the sky. They all seem to move, as if they are slowly falling toward me. Or maybe it's me, I think, who is falling toward them.

It's too cold this morning to stand still for long. I hear my father slide open the door to the barn, and once again I have to run to catch up. I am beside him as he goes through the doorway into the stable and clicks on the lights.

One or two of the cows jump as if startled when the lights go on, and I wonder if they were dreaming, too. Their tags jingle even louder now—a chorus of little bells—as the cows shift in their places, and some that were lying down slowly stand up.

At all other times of the year the cows spend the nights down in the pasture. But when the night is deep winter cold like this, we keep them here in the barn where they can be warm. Every evening we bed them down with a thick layer of straw to lie on.

Most of our cows are Guernseys. They are light brown, sometimes dark brown, and have white spots.

Then there is one who is a Brown Swiss. Her milk is the richest—thick with cream. She is 14 years old, the oldest of the cows. The rest are Holsteins. They're big black and white cows that give a lot of milk.

Now three rows of cows look toward us. They know it's time for their breakfast. Each one gets a big pitchfork full of silage made late last summer from chopped green corn stalks. As my father goes around with a cart giving some to each cow, the stable fills with the smell of it—sweet, a little like fresh-mown grass, but sharp and tangy.

Then he gives each cow a smaller scoop of meal on top of the silage. The meal is made from ground-up barley and corn, mixed together and flavored with molasses. Sometimes I nibble a handful and it tastes good.

My father climbs up the steps to the hay loft, and I follow right behind him. For a moment we both disappear into darkness until his hand finds the switch for the light. I grab hold of a thick rope, a swing we made by tying it tight around one of the thick chestnut beams high above. With a running jump, I swing myself high up onto the stacked bales of hay.

Many years ago, when my father was still a baby, Grandpa built this barn. He and the men who helped him build it made a framework of huge beams. They fastened them together with wooden pegs instead of nails.

While my father throws down hay for the cows to eat and some straw for their bedding, I search for the young kittens I know must be here somewhere.

The mother cat comes walking out from behind a bale and rubs against my legs.

"Where did you hide the kittens?" I say as I kneel down to pet her. She just smiles and continues rubbing back and forth against me.

The last bale hits the floor below with a thump and we head back downstairs.

My father carries four bales over to the center aisle while I drag first one and then another down the side aisles. I drop the second bale and begin to pull off the strings that hold it tight. It falls open into chunks like a loaf of sliced bread falls apart without its wrapper.

"Give each one a couple of chunks," Pop says.

The cows lean forward in anticipation. As each one gets her hay, she grabs it in her mouth and tosses her head from side to side to break apart the tightly packed chunk.

Dust flies everywhere and a cloud forms behind me as I walk down the row. I have to move quickly or I'll soon be covered with hay from head to foot.

My father goes to get the milkers and I walk over to the last cow in the row, a dark red-brown Guernsey.

She is one of my favorites but she has no name. There are some cows we have given names to–Princess Buttercup, Shorty, and Reds. But it is easier just to call them by their numbers and so she is Number 28.

I rub my hand along her side and reach up high to wrap my arms around her shoulders. At my touch she shivers and a big shrug ripples down the length of her back. I lean my head against her side and feel her hair soft on my cheek.

I look for my father, and seeing that he is half the barn away, I begin to talk to her. I don't want my father to know I talk to the cows. He understands a lot of things, but he wouldn't understand about this. I talk to them a lot—they are such good listeners. And Number 28, so calm and gentle, is one of the best.

"I had a dream this morning," I say to her. As I scratch the back of her head, she flips one of her ears back and forth. Then she turns as if to hear me better.

But before I can finish the story, my father throws the switch on the motor that runs the milkers, and it comes on with a deep growl.

He heads down the walkway behind the first row of cows and I run over to be next to him.

While he puts the milkers on the first cow, he says to me, "Wash off Number 3, would you?"

The milkers start up with a "Swish, swish…Swish, swish" as milk begins flowing through the clear plastic hose.

I grab a wash cloth and step between the next two cows, rubbing my hand over the back of each so they'll know I'm there.

When I've finished, I get a tin cup and squirt some milk in it for the cats that are gathered on the steps waiting for their breakfast.

The mother cat is here with the kittens I was searching for earlier. They are wrestling on the floor now and look like a ball of gray-and-black-striped fur.

They jump apart as I approach, look at me with eyes wide and then shoot up the stairs. I pour the milk into the cat dish and as the older cats lap it up, I walk over to the windows.

Each window pane is covered with lace made of snowy white frost. There are beautiful crystals and starbursts and long swooping curls.

I stare at the patterns, knowing they will soon melt and there's no way I can save them. For a moment it makes me sad.

Then I turn and watch as the cows chew the last of their hay. I want to soak it all in with my eyes, to make a memory so strong it will never leave me.

I try to stop time. I stand as still as I can, tensing every muscle in my body, even holding my breath. But it doesn't work. Time refuses to stop.

I walk back to my father and together we go down the rows, working with a rhythm like a dance we have practiced many times.

Some mornings, like this one, we are quiet as we move from cow to cow, but sometimes we talk, and sometimes he tells me stories.

For as long as I can remember, my mother and father—and my grandfather, when he was living—have told stories, stories like songs, so magical and so beautiful that you want to hear them over and over—like favorite songs on the radio you can't wait to hear again.

My father tells my sister and me stories about growing up here on the farm. My mother tells us stories about when she was growing up on her father's farm—a farm I can just barely see when I look out across the fields. And then they both tell stories about our grandparents and great-grandparents who once lived here too.

I have heard these stories so often that they are almost like my own memories. And sometimes it seems as if there is no time here, as if I could go around a corner of the barn and find my grandfather hitching up his horse to the wagon, or walk into the house and find my great-grandmother peeling apples in the kitchen.

My father and I move from one cow to the next. After each one, he stops to dump the full milker into a strainer sitting on top of a big milk can. And if I am standing close, I can smell the sweet smell of the milk, still warm from the cow.

Then finally we are done. My father takes the milker off the last cow, opens it up and pours out some milk for the cats. In spite of the little snacks I have given them, this is what they've been waiting for.

They jump down from the stairs and drink till the bowl is empty, then sit a few feet away and clean the milk from their whiskers.

My father turns off the motor and everything is quiet again except for the jingling sounds when the cows shake their heads.

While he puts the milkers to soak in hot sudsy water, I let the cows out to spend the daylight hours in the upper pasture.

Then we head toward the house. By now the stars have all melted into the pink-gray light of morning, and as we walk along, my father begins a story.

"Years ago," he says, "we had a horse named Dan. And Dan would always pull the wagon to take the milk down to the dairy.

"I would load up the wagon in the morning and while I'd go inside to eat, Dan would stand right here and wait," he says as we come to a corner of the road. "As soon as I would come outside after breakfast, Dan would hear the door slam, turn and head up the lane with the wagon and I would run and jump on.

"Well, one morning someone else must have gone out the door while I was still eating breakfast and Dan heard that slam and took off. When I got outside Dan and the wagon loaded with milk were gone.

"I hopped in the car and tore down to the dairy. And there was Dan standing in line with all the rest of the wagons. As the next wagon in line moved up Dan would move up another space–just as he did every morning.

"I got on the wagon and emptied out the milk, then turned Dan around and pointed him back toward the farm. He took off again and I followed him home in the car.

"Now that was one smart horse."

We both laugh at the story as he opens the door. Inside, Mom has breakfast cooking and I can smell maple syrup and pancakes before I get to the kitchen.

I watch my mother pour batter onto the sizzling griddle and turn the cakes as they start to bubble. My sister takes the plates out of the cupboard and sets the table.

Again I wish I could stop time and hold onto everything here forever. And again it makes me sad.

I sit down at the table and my father starts telling another story about Dan. I watch my father and there is a light in his eyes as if he can still see Dan running across the field.

Suddenly I realize that my father knows the answer–my mother, my grandfather, too–they all knew the answer, the way to stop time. It's been right in front of me and I've been listening to it all of my life. They took the things they loved and turned them into stories.

"Hey, Pop?" I say when my father finishes his story. "Back when you were little? Did you get up early to help Grandpa milk the cows?"